Deborah's Tree

For BDG—"Raise the tent peg, Barbara!"
—J.Y.

Author's Note

The story of Deborah, the first woman judge in Israel, is found in the Torah in Judges 4–5 where she is seen as a prophet, a national leader, and a military commander in the war against the invading Canaanites. As a woman, she was not allowed to have men who were not in her tribe or her family in her house, unattended, so she rendered her legal judgments under a tree near her house, which also emphasized that her judgments were open and fair. In the forty years of peace after the war, she continued as a leader, judge, and—it is said—a creator and singer of songs.

KAR-BEN PUBLISHING®
An imprint of Lerner Publishing Group, Inc.
241 First Avenue North
Minneapolis, MN 55401 USA

Website address: www.karben.com

Main body text set in Perpetua MT Std.
Typeface provided by Monotype Typography.

Library of Congress Cataloging-in-Publication Data

Names: Yolen, Jane, author. | Kawa, Cosei, illustrator.
Title: Deborah's tree / by Jane Yolen ; illustrated by Cosei Kawa.
Description: Minneapolis, MN : Kar-Ben Publishing, an imprint of Lerner Publishing Group, Inc., [2022] | Audience: Ages 5–9 | Audience: Grades 2–3 | Summary: Deborah, the first woman judge in Israel, foresees danger to the people of Israel, and helps general Barak lead his troops to victory.
Identifiers: LCCN 2021044064 (print) | LCCN 2021044065 (ebook) | ISBN 9781728438955 (library binding) | ISBN 9781728439013 (paperback) | ISBN 9781728461045 (ebook)
Subjects: LCSH: Deborah (Biblical judge)—Juvenile fiction. | CYAC: Deborah (Biblical judge)—Fiction. | Jews—History—1200-953 B.C.—Fiction.
Classification: LCC PZ7.Y78 Db 2022 (print) | LCC PZ7.Y78 (ebook) | DDC [E]—dc23

LC record available at https://lccn.loc.gov/2021044064
LC ebook record available at https://lccn.loc.gov/2021044065

Manufactured in the United States of America
1-49732-49635-1/14/2022

Deborah's Tree

By Jane Yolen
Illustrated by Cosei Kawa

KAR-BEN
PUBLISHING

Deborah is a baby.
She is asleep
on a shawl under a palm tree
near the tent.
Her mother sings a psalm.
"Let there be light.
Let there be dreams.
God, I give this child into your keeping."

Deborah is five, sitting under the palm tree,
chewing on a sweet date.
Her thoughts in the mist,
she sees the future.
"It is a gift," her father says.

But to Deborah, this seeing forward
is sometimes frightening,
sometimes a burden.

Deborah is ten,
sitting under the palm tree.
Heat rises around her like the dust
of a hundred horses, a thousand camels,
crossing the desert.

In her far-sight she sees
a chariot with something like spears
or swords on its wheels.
She turns to look behind her.
Nothing is there but a lizard,
its dark eyes a mirror
of Deborah's fear.

Deborah is twelve.
She is tall;
the date palm is taller.
Her mother lives in a small house now.
The tent is for guests
or meetings
or for travelers.

Deborah stands by the tree
picking sweet dates.
She takes the full bowl
back to the house to help Mama
make a dessert.
She has already gathered the honey.
There is no more talk of dreams
as her own future unfolds before her.

Now Deborah is a new wife
with a husband named Lapidot,
who makes lanterns and lights.
She has her own date palm—
indeed, a grove of palm trees.
She loves the feel of the tree
at her back as she sits and studies the law.

Now Deborah is a judge in Israel.
Not just a daughter, not just a wife,
but the first woman judge.
Because of how well she knows the law,
because she can sometimes see into the future.

Men come to Deborah's tree
with their concerns,
to listen to her wisdom
about buying land, about proper marriages,
about how Israel is perhaps
being punished by God
for behaving badly.
She sits in judgment under her palm tree,
where the dreams still come.

In one dream she sees a tall man
walking toward her.
It is not her husband, Lapidot,
who is smaller and with a happier face.
This man is tall.
He walks like a soldier,
shoulders broad, head high.
There is a scowl on his face.

In her dream, he disappears into the mist.
She will not worry about him,
nor will she forget him.
She will meet him in time.

The men who gather at the tree
ask Deborah to write
to the general of their army,
for there is an enemy on their border,
large, well-armed.

Deborah is the judge.
It is her job to listen to those
who come to her for advice
under her palm tree.

The sky stares down
at Deborah,
a small woman
under a tall tree.

But she is not small in heart.
Not small in honor.
Not small in God's eyes.
She writes to Barak, the general,
and asks him to come to talk with her
under the palm tree.

Barak has heard of her far-seeing, and comes.
He is a tall man, shoulders broad, head high.
He walks like a soldier. On his face is a scowl.
She remembers him well,
though they have not met.
He says, "We will fight, Judge Deborah,
but it is you who must lead the men.
They trust you."

"If I do as you ask," she tells him,
"they will say a woman—not
you—has won the war."

He smiles sadly, a man who has given
his life to his people.
"As long you have seen our victory,"
he says, "I am at ease."
"Dreams are only dreams," she
warns him.
"God does not speak directly,
but in mystery."

She tells him the future she has seen:
chariots with steel spears on their wheels.
His men prepare for that.

She asks him to pray.
"All men pray before battle," he says.
"Even the enemy."

Deborah, the baby under the palm tree,
the girl under the palm tree,
the wife under the palm tree,
the judge under the palm tree,
looks into the future once more.
But she sees nothing.
And so she knows the time
she has dreamed about
has come,
the time that God has shown her.
"This is *our* time," she says to Barak.
"The victory is ours."

And it is.